BEAST FRIENDS FOREVER!

Animal Lovers in Rhyme

BEAST FRIENDS FOREVER!

Animal Lovers in Rhyme

By Robert L. Forbes

Drawings by
Ronald Searle

Overlook Duckworth
New York · London

First published in the United States in 2013 by
Overlook Duckworth, Peter Mayer Publishers, Inc.
New York and London

NEW YORK:
141 Wooster Street
New York, NY 10012
www.overlook.com

LONDON:
Duckworth & Co. Ltd.
Greenhill House
90-93 Cowcross Street
London EC1M 6BF
www.ducknet.co.uk

Text has been set in ITC Berekley

Cataloging-in-Publication Data is available from the Library of Congress.

Book design and type formatting by Bernard Schleifer
Manufactured in China
1 3 5 7 9 8 6 4 2
ISBN 978-1-59020-808-3 (US)
ISBN 978-0-71564-403-4 (UK)

For Ronald and Monica Searle,
with a Feast of Love and Gratitude

CONTENTS

BEAST FRIENDS FOREVER!

Animal Lovers in Rhyme

Babette's Scent

Babette the Skunk adores fine perfume
And teaches young skunklettes the best way to groom,
For soon they'll grow up and want to go play
With game skunky guys for a sniff and a spray.

She's studied her art with Parisian perfumers
To pursue out the truths in those naughty French rumors
Of how to mix flowers and herbs in a potion
That floridly stirs up torrid emotion.

She gave it a name that's a little risqué –
(To help with seduction the true Français way)
Packaged in black and called "In-d-scent,"
It's sure to enflame any white-striped gent.

Now skunky ladies all through the woods
Are armed for amour with oderous goods.
The skunk world is thriving, thanks to Babette!
(There's also cologne and an eau de toilette.)

The Raccoons' Riddle

Two raccoons, Liz and Rick,
Wanted so to marry
That when they felt an instant click
They knew they couldn't tarry.

Rick, a riddler, said to Liz,
"It's really now or never
For us to have that bond which is
First, last and forever."

"What is that, my Wiz? Said Liz.
Rick smiled and said, "Just this:
We shouldn't make it very quick,
My love – 'tis our very first kiss.

"We have it only once you see,
The first, once done, is over.
It's last because, for you and me,
We'll take no other lover."

"I have you and you have me
And that won't change, not ever.
My clever Rick, you've made me see
Why first is last forever."

Dick crooned, "It's up to us, fair Liz,
To make love permanent.
We'll light a star with each new kiss –
Let's start our firmament!"

The Peacock

My peacock friend Stan
Knows just when
To display his fan
For a cute pea hen.

With that grand fan
Stan's quite the man
And fans hen's flames
As only Stan can.

Pea dames are drab
So they think Stan's fab.
They're his fan club,
You could say.
He's got a way
With his display,
And when he calls, they
Are in his sway
By day,
And night.

Adder Attraction

Until Snowball met Puff
Her adder life lacked enough
Heat. She was naturally cold blooded.
She yearned for love's blush
With its heart thumping rush
So her veins with a warm flush would be flooded.

"Dear Snowball," said Puff shyly
"I think we might be highly
Suited! Like you my temperature is underheated.
So if we get entwined,
Our friction, when combined
With love, lets our snaky natures be completed.

Thrushes

The trills that cascade through the pipes of his throat
Are thrilling enough for the Wood Thrush to gloat,
Though not always can he the top song bird be.
There's a forest rival more melodic than he,
His not-distant cousin, the rare Hermit Thrush,
Whose silvery symphony makes the woods hush,
But even the Hermit must strive to be better,
For his songs to his true love don't always get her.

Elephant Eloquence

The call of a young mister elephant
To us doesn't seem very elegant;
But oh for young maiden elephants,
The sound is sweet-honeyed eloquence.

Lancelot the Ocelot

Lancelot the Ocelot is caged and doing time.
His romance turned to tragedy, ending in a crime,
A crime of passion, surely, but was Lance, alone, to blame?
He fell in love with his best friend's wife, Gwenny was her name.
And when King Art, her husband, with only love to give,
Discovered their unfatihfulness, he lost the will to live.

The ocelots, a brotherhood, had sought to rule the vale
With goodness and compassion, these woods their holy grail.
But Art went off to hunt one day to seek a quieter place
Where Ocelots could raise their tots and flee the human race,
For man was cruelly tearing down their sylvan Camelot,
Here putting up a shopping mall, and there, a parking lot.

Good Art's fey sis, Morgana, was the source of all this ill —
She'd sold out to a cat named Tromp — oh, what a bitter pill! —
Because the lass was envious of svelte Gwenn's spotted pelt
And hated what she couldn't have — mad jealousy she felt.

Morgana cast a wicked spell so Gwenn's undying pledge
To Art was dimmed, her heart confused, and she was on the edge
Of dying when good Lancelot arrived to help the wife
Of his best friend and sworn liege lord, prepared to give his life.
Instead, a love between them flared that had a mournful end.

When Art returned to fetch the band, he sadly found his friend
Had betrayed their deepest trust, all honor now was smashed;
He fought a duel with Lancelot but knew his hopes were dashed.
Art saw his life was running out and let a fatal blow
Pierce his heart, as Lance cried out, beholding the King's blood flow,
"Oh, Art, my lord, what have I done? I never meant for this
To be your fate or mine or Gwenn's!" And gave him a final kiss.

Now scattered o'er the thinning woods, the Ocelot band was done.
A hunter killed the grieving Gwenn with one shot from his gun.
Proud Lancelot was rounded up and put on bold display
For all to see his treachery, though some will surely say,
"It's not his fault!" and point to her who fated the awful deed,
Morgana in her jewels and fur, the strutting queen of greed,
Now the pampered pet of him who built the parking lot,
Who has the gall to dub his mall, — yes, call it Camelot.

Groovy Doobie

I know a Blue-footed Booby,
A goofy young punkster named Doobie
Who dyed his feet red to be groovy
And at night plays blues on his toobie
Which is brassy and loud
For the teenybooby crowd,
So when he toodles by,
The girls all cry,
"Let me be your baby Booby, groovy Doobie!"

Lee the Hero

A brave meerkat named Lee
Is no mere cuddly kitty.
He told me he prefers to be
The daredevil in my ditty.

He loves a good fight
With a flashing sword or gun,
But scratching and biting
Are also sharp fun.

Off he'll dash on a risky rescue
Of a meerkat maid in distress
If only to hear a whispered "Bless you,"
And catch a chaste kiss, no more or less.

A gallant gent, our valiant Lee,
Full of dash and daring,
He chases after enemies
Or pirates while seafaring.

But it's bedtime after dinner,
So Lee goes without a fuss,
Laying down sword and dagger,
Unloading his blunderbuss.

Tomorrow he'll be up with zest,
Villains to follow, promises to keep,
But now to rest before those quests —
Hero meerkats need their sleep.

Squig

I know a pig whose name is Squig
Who's very fat and squat and big.
It's not enough to be just round,
So he sports hair that brushes the ground,
Whistling, bristling, swooshing around, with a
Whisha-whasha, whisha-whasha, whasha-whisha.

Squig's so hairy that you don't know
Which end is stop and which is go.
The go end has a pudgy pink snout
Under floppy pink ears that barely poke out,
While he oinks his love-songs, barrelling about, with a
Gerronka-gerronka, gerronka-gerroink.

This big bushy boar is so manly and cool
That all the piggy missies eye him and drool
Even forgetting the slops in their trough,
Squealing, "Squiggy, my man! Never cut that hair off!"
Each yearns for a cuddle in a sty warm and soft, with a
Squiggy-wiggy wrigglely! Ooh Squiggy-wriggely wiggy!

But it's tough to be a rock-star pig
With groupie-piggies galore jamming each gig.
So Squig dreams of a sow to share his fate
To be his big squeeze, and procreate,
Who'll love every pound and be his sweet mate, with a
Wowee, soowee, sooowee, wowee!

Bugsie Seagull

When it dawned on Bugsie he was bored with home —
The beach, the sand, the waves, the foam,
The squawling kids and soggy french fries —
He spread his wings, said his goodbyes
And left Cape Cod, flying due west,
Searching by day, while at night he'd rest.

Deep inland he awoke to a soothing hymn,
The cooing of a morning dove seduced him.
In rustling woods where the shade is deep,
They built a nest, with promises to keep.

Now they're raising a brood in the pines —
Not one of Mother Nature's predictable designs:
A seagull in the forest with a morning dove.
But it pays to take a chance on love
For if you don't, you may never know
What joy awaits you, how far you can go,
So take a bold step, in spite of your genes,
And remember Bugsie — follow your dreams!

Tri-Humphal Kim

For my friend the camel named Kim
The future looked boring and grim
'Til the camel committee
Of Dromedary City
Gave three humps, not two, to him.

He now makes a very good living
Happily always out giving
To husbands and wives
The rides of their lives!
Oh, the delight Kim's delivering!

Dapper Don's Foxtrot

Dapper Don the Dancer
Told me the other day
Of a confusing dilemma
That refuses to go away.

As a fox, he's snappily clever,
With moves smooth and fleet,
So when he's giving lessons,
He sweeps ladies off their feet.

At the swing, Don is a master;
His jive is mesmerizing;
His quick-step's even faster,
And his salsa hotly surprising.

His waltz is totally tidal
With a pull that rivals the moon,
Making ladies feel alive and vital,
Swirling them into a swoon.

With swaying hips in the cha-cha
His flying feet fairly hover,
While his electric cucaracha
Is 100% Latin lover.

Don slinks a sultry bolero,
Dips and dives in his torchy tango;
He's a dervish at the devilish mambo,
Lighting sparks with a flirty fandango.

"That's why it's so curious,"
He sadly said to me,
"I try not to get upset or furious
But it's humiliating, you see.

"My students notice how I bumble...
I have to tell them that I cannot...
I trip, stumble and fumble...
But I just can't do the *foxtrot*!

"Don't laugh! I know it's not normal
As a master of ballroom dance
To have no foxtrot, the natural
Choreography of romance."

"You're smart!" I wisely advised,
"Instead of being annoyed,
You have rightly realized
That your skill-set has a small void.

"I agree that nature is cruel,
You can't do everything perfectly;
Just hire for the Dapper Don School
Someone who can foxtrot expertly."

He searched for the perfect instructor
And when he finally got her,
Was so besotted he had to conduct her
Down the aisle, his soulmate fox-trotter.

Don and Dawn these days are thriving —
The school is swingingly busy,
While at night with their cubs they are jiving
In fun family conga line tizzy!

Why Lena Cries

The first time I met Lena
She was an average girl hyena
Who could laugh right on cue
Because that's what hyenas do.
The Animal Cliché League is pretty strict:
Hyenas must laugh, so goes the edict.

But Lena read a book called, *Anna,*
Hyena Queen of the Savannah,
A historical page-turning gripper,
Part bio, part bodice-ripper
About castles, lace and swordfights
And how Anna's liege lord fights
For her honor, love and a kiss.
Nary a chapter would Anna miss.
Miracles happen to make hearts throb,
All producing a sniffle, then a sob,
Heaving, sighing, there's no denying
These tales leave Lena…crying!

The ACL then got stricter
And decided they'd have to evict her,
Our Lena, for not being correct,
For not doing what they expect.
Now she can't run with the pack
And must always hang back.
But not once did she ever come pleading
As she'd actually rather be reading
More blazing stories of brave Anna
And passions aroused on the savannah.

So when you're next out on safari,
And the night falls, you shouldn't worry
When the hyenas start laughing aloud
And one sound stands out from the crowd —
Another Savannah Anna tall tale
Has made a lonely hyena wail
Her pitiful, heart wrenching boo-hoo.
Yes, you've guessed: it's you know who.

Honey and Sweets

Honey and Sweets
Are two parakeets
I bought because they were big talkers.
In the rowdy bird crowd,
They chirruped most loud,
So I thought I'd have fun with these squawkers.

But once out of the shop
Their chatter did stop —
By love they were hopelessly bitten.
My songsters won't tweet,
Now they're lovebirds discreet,
Cooing soft woo, so heartily smitten.

Flannery and his Irish Wolfhound

Flannery was a hard-boiled Louse
Whose bad behavior got him bounced from the house.
Homeless, he landed on a mangy wolfhound,
Where unlikely true love he found.

He fell fully and totally, if unmannerly
For this shaggy she-dog, our Flannery,
Which meant he moved right in,
Digging his love-nest just under her skin.

When the bug was snug, he met some fellow lice
Who also found the wolfhound's pelt nice.
They'd gather at the local pub,
Belting love songs 'til they'd blub.

But now imagine, if you will,
Our poor hound who'd had her fill
Of this louse and his love bites
That made for itchy days and nights.

The dear girl howled and rolled and rubbed
And even submitted to being bath-tubbed.
She had no clue, not even slight
That she was adored by her parasite.

With all her scratching, Flannery came to see
That this romance wasn't meant to be.
Because her happiness was his aim
He sadly decided to change his game.

To his louse pals, he said, "Adieu.
With unrequited love I'm through.
Please join me in my about-face
As I unleash her from my mad embrace.
Let's all hop off so she will be
Not writhing in irritated misery."
So they hopped on to other pets —
Will Flannery again find love? I'm taking bets!

Mellow and Marcello

A doe gazelle named Mellow
Went out with a fast buck named Marcello,
Galloping over the plain,
Parched dry due to lack of rain,
Kicking up billows of dust
Which got the geezers all fussed,
Who shouted, "Whoa, Marcello, slow down!
Mellow, watch who you hang around!"

But Mellow didn't heed or care
As the two zoomed by on a tear,
Past fat cats who would have liked to eat them,
But even the leopard couldn't beat them.

The dry spell was getting longer,
With the African sun beating down stronger
When those two started a new race
At a dust-raising hurricane pace,
Stirring clouds that soon filled the sky
Leaving the sun wondering, "Why should I
Try so hard to fry the earth, it
Is for now just not worth it."

At the sun's relaxing, the air cooled a bit
And the rain clouds thought, "This is it!
At long last, it's our turn to play!
We'll send a load of drops earth's way!"

So they let loose a drenching shower
And within one joyful hour
The wetted cloud of kicked-up dust
Swirled and reddened like deep rust
So that creatures everywhere
Were muddied in their skin and hair.
Life-giving rain, down it poured;
Dry spirits of the plain once again soared.

Mellow and Marcello were finally slowed,
The strain of their pace and their muscles
    showed;
They lay down to gather their waning
    strength
To repose, to think, to drink, at length.
As they guzzled, they sweetly nuzzled
Nose to nose, showing the herd
That whirlwind love can be the final word.

Down At The Old Mill Inn

My pal Walter's Head Waiter at The Old Mill Inn
Where guys and dolls come nights for music and dancing,
A taste of heaven, an earthy brush with sin,
In alcoves perfect for tête-à-tête romancing.

Walter knows the ways of his river crowd,
Who sits where and who must have front row tables,
Like the Beaver kingpins, oh-so proud
Of their Muskrat dames dripping jewels and sables.

Walter checks to see who's in the flow,
As valets unctuously park the Rolls
That have brought a bevy of younger beaux
Escorting the old divorcee Voles.

Weeknights aren't late but steady,
While the Saturday Soiree has them all flocking
For the big band sound and songs of Eddy
And The Otter Khans — the joint gets rocking.

Walter holds a table for VIPs just in case
Frankie the River Rat and his pack decide
To show up, or her sleekness, La Lola Grace
(Miss Mink of some time ago) takes a slide

Downstream for a mix of flirtation and cocktails.
Or in struts Douglas Ferret of stage and screen,
Tanned, pomaded, in top hat and tails
To charm some preening young thing into a casting scene.

Walter's seen it all — his whiskers are quick to twitch at trouble,
Like the time David Copperhead took offense
At Louie the Lounge Lizard who'd ordered a double
Snake juice but spat it out, and made the crowd tense

When he said he'd spit at "snake anything,"
Clearly oiled, roiled and spoiling for a fight.
So Walter gave the bar bell a little ding,
Signaling Biff the Bouncer to fling that cad into the night.

By the way, the eats at the Old Mill Inn are tasty, too,
With portions generous to a fault.
So the next time you're down the river why don't you
Stop in and give my regards to the great Mr. Walt.

Grizzly Rose's Snores

Rose the Grizzly's noisy nose
Is quite an instrument.
From it floats a storm of notes
That pierce the firmament.
High tones shudder,
Mid snorts judder
And deep growls thunder and bellow.

Throughout the cave they resonate,
Making it hard to hibernate!

But to Rose's adoring fellow
The vigorous snoring
And snootful roaring
Of his lovely lady bear,
Reassure him she's there
And that their love is alive,
So though he's sleep-deprived,
Her snores keep her big fellow mellow.

Nights of the Iguanas

Juana and Anna live in my yard,
Leathery iguanas who try very hard
To find a fine fella by cruising the bars,
A hunky Goodzilla for a ride to the stars.

It's hot in the sun so their taste runs to skimpy
(Those minis and tube tops are daringly shrimpy!).
They flicker their tongues and act lizard-coy,
Hoping to lure a cool cold-blooded boy.

Their goal is to settle in thick leafy hedges
To raise scaly babies who'll sun on the ledges
While they reminisce with stars in their eyes
About chasing Goodzillas, those charming green guys.

The Rich Cow Daisy

Daisy always had money because her dad was tops in the market.
He left her his wealth, but it was a burden most dark. It
Gave her airs as a heifer.

And as a young bovine, she thought her gold would be love's spark
But it turned out to be a curse, and worse, it attracted a bold shark,
Who won her heart then left her

When he got enough of her dough, so you'd think she'd learn
Life's balance and joys come from what you do and earn.
With self worth, anything you can weather.

Her moolah was the only thing on which Daisy could depend,
So she ended up old and tough and yet, useful in the end
As shoes of leather.

Why the Kookaburra Laughs

The Kookaburra named Oz
Lives at the local zoo
And loves it there because
There is always plenty to do.

Oz grew up Down Under
But found it too quiet and rural.
In contrast, zoo life's a wonder,
A riotous social whirl.

All day, humans troop by his cage,
A parade that's ever so funny,
Of every description and age,
And some even like to toss money.

Come nightfall, he's at the zoo casino
With buddy birds gathered for poker
Where he won a big hand against Dino
With three kings, two queens and a joker.

So he decked out his pad with nice things
That attracted a home girl named Laura.
What style to his life she now brings,
Such a lovely, old fashioned aura.

With his wife he now watches as you
And your unfeathered family stroll by
Which makes them laugh, "Kooka-koo, Koo,
Kooka-koo-koo, Koo-kye!"

The Python

My friend Monty is a naughty python
Who met his wife in a python pile-on.
When she emerged she had his pant on
And he, blushing, had her nylon on.

Cricket Noise

I know a cricket
Over there in the thicket
Whose habit is making
Cricket noise.
He once tried to kick it
But found it's the right ticket,
For that noise
Leads cricket girls
To cricket boys.

Jim the Gym Rat

Slim Jim was a rat who worked at the lab
Where they fattened him up to study his flab
But this got drab so he fled to the gym,
And now I will tell you what happened to him.

He worked like a fiend to abolish his fat,
Getting buffed and defined and polished — all that.
He would only wear the most form-fitting clothes
That show off your muscles, as everyone knows,
But he never passed up a long look in a mirror
To check his reflection as perfection got nearer.

A babe rat named Jenna, gym-pumped like him
Caught the eye (in a mirror) of Iron Rat Jim.
They worked out together, getting vainer and vainer
And after a week, they were wed by their trainer.
But when they went out for a honeymoon walk
Both rodents discovered they'd rather not talk.

They had nothing to say so headed back in
To share their obsession with staying trim-thin.
They chiseled their delts and carved their sleek lats
And refined their fine abs not to six- but eight-packs.

Here is the sad part: Jim started to feel
That this rat race of gym life was less than ideal.
His wife was an image, their life an illusion.
They had no real marriage, no physical fusion.

He started to reach out to Jenna to say
That he felt body sculpting held way too much sway.
As he walked over, he took a last glance
At himself in the mirror but just then by chance
He tripped, stumbled and tumbled on his head,
Which cracked open, leaving him dead.

How ironic life is — he went back to the lab,
A bionic specimen, cold on a slab.
The place he escaped from, so dry and so drab.
No scientists there remember Jim's flab.

Jenna never hung up her pink-sparkly spandex,
Still gym-trimming with no thought for her dead-ex.
So, caution when you join the Narcissus Gym —
Just remember Jim's Missus, and what happened to him.

69

Juliette and Her Suitors

She certainly was a beautiful bird,
Juliette.
Her father was a Spanish prince,
Her mother a dazzler of the Paris stage.
One night after her bow
The prince made her a vow
That he would show her how
To be happy if they left now,
For Rio,
Where they've been happy ever since.

Alas, they had only one child
But she had enough energy for three.
At a precocious age
She left her gilded cage
And like her Maman
Became all the rage,
A bright star on the stage,
Driving the crowds wild.

Oh, what a handful as she got older,
Especially as a teen.
Headstrong and free,
She liked to fly around and see
Boys line up for her, like soldiers.
She would pick three
To kiss and tease,
Or peck them if they got bolder.

Truly, Juliette
Was the prettiest Scarlet Macaw
Who ever set wings and hearts a-flutter.
On her branch she could be seen
Fluffing her feathers like a queen,
Strutting, preening —
To her suitors, plain mean,
But they'd take it, flapping around her tree in awe.

All this flirtation, though, left Juliette cold.
Will she ever find someone strong
Enough to love her, a prince like her father?
With the right words to utter,
To melt her like butter?
But her hapless suitors could only seem to stutter
Or mumble, or flap and flutter.
Not a single one did she find pleasingly bold.

Until one day there appeared a Toucan.
Ferdinand was different from the rest:
Black feathers, a puffed out breast,
A yellow beak, manly and sleek,
Not a timid suitor or horn tooter
But a Don Juan of the Amazon
Who'd learned love's prime protocol:
"I'll play it cool. That's my rule.
I'll win her. I know I can."

So at first he gave Juliette the cold shoulder
And flirted with her maids,
Invading their quarters for kissing raids.
This of course incensed her,
Made her smolder. She fenced right back,
Spurned him as a cad,
Held herself aloof, though secretly waiting
For some real proof
Of his devotion,
Some real emotion, bigger, bolder.

Refusing to give in, to bow
To her will,
Ferdinand wore down Juliette's pride
Until one day she cried,
"We have to stop playing!
This act is so dismaying!
Enough delaying!
If you make me a vow,
My Toucan prince,
I'll show you how
We can be happy right now!"

Those were the magic words,
To stop their silly row.
He made her a heartfelt promise,
Sealed it with a kiss,
And they've been two happy birds
Ever since!

A Kestrel Couple

My Elize
On the breeze
Through the trees
To our nest
In flighting
Exciting
Kestrel kiting
Now alighting
From our quest.

Squirmy worms
Earth affirms
Eager squeaks,
Mewling mood
Foraged food
Feeds the brood
Fast chewed
In cheeky beaks.

Timeless honor
Father, mother,
Eye-closed lives
Lovesong sung
Heartmate won
Spring sprung
Eggs done —
Nature thrives.

About the Author

"He spends a lot of time looking out the window," read one of Robert Forbes' 7th grade report cards. Even so, he managed to graduate from school and university, and joined the family business in 1975 where he now serves as a company Vice President as well as President of the lifestyle magazine, *ForbesLife*. After 25 years in New York City and six in London, he and his wife currently reside in Palm Beach, Florida. He enjoys his work, writing poetry, and still cherishes time spent looking out windows. His first two books of poetry for children, *BEASTLY FEASTS! – A Mischievous Menagerie in Rhyme* and *LET'S HAVE A BITE! – A Banquet of Beastly Rhymes*, are also illustrated by Ronald Searle.

About the Illustrator

Ronald Searle was born in Cambridge in 1920. He served in the Second World War and was one of the few British prisoners-of-war to survive Changi prison and forced labor on the Burma Railway. He delighted millions with his comic creation St. Trinians, and has been a distinguished contributor to numerous magazines around the world, from *The New Yorker* to *Le Monde*. Searle sadly died in December of 2011 but the drawings for this book happily were completed a while ago.